# I Got the School Spirit

Connie Schofield-Morrison · ILLUSTRATED BY Frank Morrison

BLOOMSBURY
CHILDREN'S BOOKS
NEW YORK  LONDON  OXFORD  NEW DELHI  SYDNEY

To all the students at the School by the Sea PS43MS and
all the students who have the school spirit worldwide
—C. S.-M.

To my youngest daughter, Tiffani. Continue hopping,
skipping, and jumping toward your dreams. Dad.
—F. M.

BLOOMSBURY CHILDREN'S BOOKS
Bloomsbury Publishing Inc., part of Bloomsbury Publishing Plc
1385 Broadway, New York, NY 10018

BLOOMSBURY, BLOOMSBURY CHILDREN'S BOOKS, and the Diana logo are trademarks of Bloomsbury Publishing Plc

First published in the United States of America in July 2020
by Bloomsbury Children's Books

Bloomsbury books may be purchased for business or promotional use. For information on bulk purchases please contact
Macmillan Corporate and Premium Sales Department at specialmarkets@macmillan.com

Library of Congress Cataloging-in-Publication Data
Names: Schofield-Morrison, Connie, author. | Morrison, Frank, illustrator.
Title: I got the school spirit / by Connie Schofield-Morrison ; illustrated by Frank Morrison.
Description: [New York] : Bloomsbury Children's Books, 2020.
Summary: As a new school year begins, a young girl is filled with school spirit as she zips her book bag shut, rides the bus, enjoys her
classes, and eagerly anticipates the next day.
Identifiers: LCCN 2019044657 (print) | LCCN 2019044658 (e-book)
ISBN 978-1-5476-0261-2 (hardcover) • ISBN 978-1-5476-0262-9 (e-book) • ISBN 978-1-5476-0263-6 (e-PDF)
Subjects: CYAC: First day of school—Fiction. | Schools—Fiction. | Enthusiasm—Fiction. | African Americans—Fiction.
Classification: LCC PZ7.S3682 Iaak 2020  (print) | LCC PZ7.S3682  (e-book) | DDC [E]—dc23
LC record available at https://lccn.loc.gov/2019044657
LC ebook record available at https://lccn.loc.gov/2019044658

Art created with oil on canvas
Typeset in Elroy and Platsch
Book design by Yelena Safronova
Printed in China by RR Donnelley, Dongguan City, Guangdong
2  4  6  8  10  9  7  5  3  1

All papers used by Bloomsbury Publishing Plc are natural, recyclable products made from wood grown in well-managed forests.
The manufacturing processes conform to the environmental regulations of the country of origin.

To find out more about our authors and books visit www.bloomsbury.com and sign up for our newsletters.

Summer is over.
My first day is here.
I got the spirit to
start the new
school year!

I slip on the spirit in my shiny new shoes.

STOMP, STOMP!

I fill up my tummy with the spirit.
Sunny-side up!

I pack my book bag with the spirit.

ZIP, ZIP!

I wait for the spirit to call my name.

HERE, HERE!

We sing the spirit loud and clear.

ABC, 123!

I kick the spirit high up in the air.

KA-POW!

I listen as the spirit weaves a story.

I jump when the spirit
splits the air!

I feel the spirit in a big ol' hug.

SQUISH,

The school spirit helps us all strive and grow.
I can't wait to see what I'll learn tomorrow!